"Bring the Classics to Life"

Metropolis

Level 5

Series Designer
Philip J. Solimene

Editor
Deborah Tiersch-Allen

EDCON

Story Adapter
Barbara Lamonica

Author
Thea von Harbou

Copyright © 1997
A/V Concepts Corp.
30 Montauk Blvd, Oakdale NY 11769
info@edconpublishing.com
1-888-553-3266
Visit our Web site at: www.edconpublishing.com

Printed in U.S.A.
ISBN# 0-931334-68-3

CONTENTS

WORDS USED

	Story 1	Story 2	Story 3	Story 4	Story 5

KEY WORDS

Story 1	Story 2	Story 3	Story 4	Story 5
boss	admission	bough	aisle	clutch
ceiling	concert	crush	invisible	dodge
clumsy	emergency	dense	mask	hasty
effort	hum	flung	pal	junk
member	melody	monster	recess	pace
purchase	musical	timber	sturdy	value

NECESSARY WORDS

Story 1	Story 2	Story 3	Story 4	Story 5
fever	restless	crystal	mass	horror
slave	limbs	sway	hissed	
skeleton	swirl		dismissed	
horrible	sweat			

WORDS USED

Story 6	Story 7	Story 8	Story 9	Story 10
KEY WORDS				
alter	chamber	bonfire	bronze	attempt
appreciate	compact	caravan	canal	breeches
capital	furious	herb	cement	chant
garment	peculiar	jewelry	conquer	dart
geography	practical	society	crumble	proper
spaghetti	system	stationary	generation	thrilling
NECESSARY WORDS				
haste	monk	mob	destruction	tattered
	sin	dome	greed	
	evil			
	shimmering			
	presence			

The Machine City

PREPARATION

Key Words

boss	(bôs, bos)	a person who tells workers what to do *The boss told the men to work faster.*
ceiling	(sē´ ling)	the inside top of a room *The light was hanging from the middle of the ceiling.*
clumsy	(klum´ zē)	not moving smoothly; awkward *The clumsy student tripped.*
effort	(ef´ ərt)	the act of trying hard *He made an effort to climb the mountain.*
member	(mem´ bər)	one who belongs to a particular group *She is a member of the Girl Scouts.*
purchase	(pėr´ chəs)	buy *You can purchase salt at the supermarket.*

The Machine City

Necessary Words

fever   (fē´ vər)   body temperature that is higher than normal
His fever kept him home from school.

slave   (slāv)   a person who is the property of another
The cruel master punished his slave for making a simple mistake.

skeleton   (skel´ ə tan)   the total of all the bones that make up a body
The students used a skeleton to learn the names and positions of the bones in the human body.

horrible   (hôr´ ə bəl)   terrible; very unpleasant
As the airplane crashed, it made a horrible noise.

People

Freder Fredersen   is a strong young man and the son of the Master of Metropolis.

Slim   is Freder's servant and guard.

Joh Fredersen   is Freder's father and the Master of Metropolis.

Places

Metropolis   is a city of the future that is controlled by a master. It relies on machines for its life.

The Club of the Sons   is a meeting place for the sons of wealthy men in Metropolis.

Eternal Gardens   are the beautiful gardens within The Club of the Sons.

New Tower of Babel   is the control center for the machine city of Metropolis.

The Machine City

A beautiful woman and a group of ragged children entered the beauty of the Eternal Gardens. Freder and his friends were forced to see the less fortunate children of Metropolis.

Preview:
1. Read the name of the story.
2. Look at the picture.
3. Read the sentences under the picture.
4. Read the first two paragraphs of the story.
5. Then answer the following question.

You learned from your preview that
_____ a. Freder was being held prisoner.
_____ b. Freder's dream was going to come true.
_____ c. Freder's dream left him feeling sad and angry.
_____ d. Freder was planning to set out on a journey.

Turn to the Comprehension Check on page 10 for the right answer.

Now read the story.

Read to find out what will happen in the Eternal Gardens.

The Machine City

Freder Fredersen was sick with fever when a dream came to him. In the dream, he heard a rumbling sound. Then the sky seemed to burst apart, and the earth, startled from her sleep, began to shake. Her rivers dried up and her mountains fell to ruin. The ground ripped open and fire sprang up. Then from the ashes rose a beautiful bird with colored wings. The bird fluttered aimlessly above the ruined earth and let out a sad cry, and Freder too, felt its sadness. Then, before his eyes, he saw a beautiful woman. He made an effort to reach out for her, but she vanished and there the dream came to an end.

Freder got up and opened the window of his workshop. He looked out upon the rumbling machine city of Metropolis. He felt a quiver run down his back and he knew that Slim, his servant, was watching him.

"I wish to be quite alone," Freder said softly. And silently, Slim left.

But Freder knew Slim would never be far away. Freder smiled an angry smile. He was a treasure to be guarded. The son of a great father must be watched carefully. His thoughts stopped again and his mind wandered back to that day in The Club of the Sons . . .

The Club of the Sons was one of the most beautiful buildings in Metropolis. And why not? For fathers, to whom every turn of the slave-run machines meant gold, could purchase anything. This building, which they had purchased for their sons, had game rooms, theaters and swimming pools. Best of all, it had the Eternal Gardens, where the servants' only job was to be always cheerful. The sons must never suspect the sadness beneath the machine city.

That day, after winning a game, Freder lazily stretched out to rest. He saw the sunlight stream through the glass ceiling above. Woman servants brought food and waited on him. From their smooth white hands, Freder ate the fruits he enjoyed.

While mixing a drink, one of the servants began to laugh, and Freder, for no reason except that he was young and happy, began to laugh. The laughter in the garden swelled to a storm as each member of the club joined in the cheerful sound. Then, suddenly, the laughter stopped. Freder turned his head. No one in the garden moved a hand or foot. They just stood and watched.

The door of the Eternal Gardens had opened, and through it came a group of ragged children. Their small faces seemed gray and old. They looked like skeletons covered with faded rags as they took clumsy steps forward on thin, bare feet.

Their leader was a beautiful woman. She stood perfectly still and gave each of the members a stern look. Then she let go of the children and stretched forward her hand.

Pointing toward the members, she said to the children, "Look, these are your brothers."

Then, pointing toward the children, she spoke to the members, "Look, these are your brothers."

She stood still, and her eyes fell on Freder. **The guards** came, but no one dared to touch her. Then she took the children by the hand, turned, and led them out.

Within the walls of marble and under the ceiling of glass there was much dismay. The guards did not know how the woman and the children had gotten inside.

Freder looked around at the Eternal Gardens and the elegant beings in it and he looked at himself. He wore the white silk and the soft, quiet shoes of all the sons. Freder looked at his friends, who never tired unless from sport, and he recalled the woman's soft words: "Look, these are your brothers." Freder felt sick. He jumped up and ran out the door in search of the mysterious woman, but no one knew who she was or from where she had come.

Freder walked home with the sounds of the machine city thumping in his head. He locked himself in his workshop, but that did not help. He kept seeing the firm but sweet face of the woman and he kept hearing her words.

Freder listened to the rumblings of the city and, for the first time, he understood the sound. The sound was beautiful and horrible. Soon, Metropolis raised her voice again. The machines of Metropolis roared because they wanted to be fed.

Freder looked across the city at the building called the New Tower of Babel. In the New Tower lived the man who was the Master of Metropolis. He was the boss who pressed his fingers to the blue metal control board so the machines of the city would roar for food. And living men were the food!

The living food would march along in lines. Men, all wearing the same dark blue pants, the same hard clumsy shoes and the same black caps, marched to the gate of The New Tower.

Past them, going the other way, another dark blue stream would drag itself along with great effort. The machine center of Metropolis would throw them up as it swallowed the others. Then the Master of Metropolis would stop pressing his fingers to the blue metal control board, and once more the endless beating of the machines could be heard.

Freder stared at the old church. It was the last building that stood as an enemy to the wicked Metropolis. The Gothics, a small but eager group, were the only people to stand against the boss of Metropolis. They would not let the church be torn down.

Suddenly, Freder was seized by the idea that he would lose his mind if he had once more to hear the machines roar to be fed. He turned from the bright lights of the city and went to speak with the Master of Metropolis, Joh Fredersen, who was his father.

The Machine City

COMPREHENSION CHECK

> **Preview Answer:**
>
> c.   Freder's dream left him feeling sad and angry.

Choose the best answer.

1. The servants in the Eternal Gardens were supposed to
   _____ a. keep everything clean.
   _____ b. buy things for the sons.
   _____ c. work at the machines.
   _____ d. be cheerful all the time.

2. While the fathers ran the city, the sons
   _____ a. went to school.
   _____ b. helped their fathers.
   _____ c. played and enjoyed themselves.
   _____ d. marched in lines to the machine center.

3. First, the woman brought the children into the Eternal Gardens. Then, the guards came. Next,
   _____ a. Freder began to laugh.
   _____ b. Freder jumped up and ran out.
   _____ c. Freder stared at the old church.
   _____ d. Freder went to sleep.

4. The faces of the children seemed
   _____ a. angry.
   _____ b. gray and old.
   _____ c. amused.
   _____ d. pink and pretty.

5. Freder wore
   _____ a. dark blue pants.
   _____ b. faded rags.
   _____ c. high leather boots.
   _____ d. white silk.

6. After he saw the woman, Freder
   _____ a. began to think there was something wrong with his city.
   _____ b. felt happier about everything.
   _____ c. joined a group called the Gothics.
   _____ d. argued with his father and left the city forever.

7. The machine workers of Metropolis
   _____ a. led happy lives.
   _____ b. were just food for the machines.
   _____ c. had games rooms, theaters, and swimming pools.
   _____ d. were all women.

8. Freder's father was
   _____ a. a servant named Slim.
   _____ b. the Master of Metropolis.
   _____ c. killed by the machines.
   _____ d. a machine worker.

9. Another name for this story could be
   _____ a. "The Eternal Gardens".
   _____ b. "Freder's Journey".
   _____ c. "Freder's City".
   _____ d. "Joh Fredersen".

10. This story is mainly about
    _____ a. a dream Freder had.
    _____ b. a beautiful woman.
    _____ c. how the city is run.
    _____ d. a city at war.

Check your answers with the key on page 67.

The Machine City

VOCABULARY CHECK

boss	ceiling	clumsy	effort	member	purchase

I. Sentences to Finish

Fill in the blank in each sentence with the correct key word from the box above.

1. Jack was afraid he was too _____ to play basketball.

2. Let's make a list of things we need to _____ for the party.

3. She was so good at her work that she became the _____ .

4. Steve is the newest _____ of the team.

5. Before we paint the walls, we have to do the _____ .

6. Alison made a great _____ to win the race.

II. Matching

Write the letter of the correct meaning from Column B next to the key word in Column A.

Column A	Column B
_____ 1. boss	a. the inside top of a room
_____ 2. ceiling	b. one who belongs to a group
_____ 3. clumsy	c. one who tells workers what to do
_____ 4. effort	d. to buy
_____ 5. member	e. act of trying hard
_____ 6. purchase	f. awkward

Check your answers with the key on page 69.

Freder's Decision

PREPARATION

Key Words

admission	(ad mish´ ən)	1. to be let in somewhere *Upon <u>admission</u>, please take your seat.* 2. the price you pay to be let in *Our <u>admission</u> to the show cost one dollar.*
concert	(kon´ sərt)	one or more musicians performing *We enjoyed listening to the piano <u>concert</u>.*
emergency	(i mėr´ jən sē)	a time of sudden trouble *In case of <u>emergency</u>, call the police.*
hum	(hum)	a sound made with the lips closed *If you don't know the words to this song, just <u>hum</u>.* an uninterrupted murmuring sound *I could hear the <u>hum</u> from the motor of the refrigerator, so I knew it was working to keep the food cold.*
melody	(mel´ ə de)	a song or the tune of a song or other piece of music *That song has a lovely <u>melody</u>.*
musical	(myü´ zə kəl)	anything having to do with music *The flute is a <u>musical</u> instrument.*

Freder's Decision

Necessary Words

restless   (rest´ lis)   rarely or never still or quiet; always moving
The restless cat chose to wander throughout the night.

limbs   (limz)   parts like arms and legs of the body
The limbs of the old tree almost touched the ground.

swirl   (swėrl)   move or drive along with a twisting position
When I pulled the plug in the tub, the water swirled down the drain.

sweat   (swet)   tiny drops of water coming through the pores of the skin
Five minutes into the race, the runner's shirt was wet with sweat.

People

Josephat   is a secretary to Joh Fredersen in the New Tower of Babel, and a new friend to Freder Fredersen.

Georgi   is worker number 11811 who runs an important machine, under the New Tower in the machine room of Metropolis.

Places

The Machine Room   is the room under the New Tower of Babel where the machines are kept.

Freder's Decision

Freder touched the arm of the worker Georgi, known as 11811. A change would come to the lives of both men.

Preview:
1. Read the name of the story.
2. Look at the picture.
3. Read the sentences under the picture.
4. Read the first four paragraphs of the story.
5. Then answer the following question.

You learned from your preview that

_____ a. the helpers were not as important as the numbers on the screen.

_____ b. Joh Fredersen was a kind man.

_____ c. the workers were paid well for their work.

_____ d. Joh Fredersen cared more for his helpers than he cared for his son.

Turn to the Comprehension Check on page 16 for the right answer.

Now read the story.

Read to find out how Freder plans to help the workers of Metropolis.

Freder's Decision

The Master of Metropolis, with eight of his helpers, sat in front of the control board. The board flashed out numbers which the helpers quickly copied into books. Joh Fredersen would then check their work with the list of the day's business figures that was before him.

"Mistake," he said, turning to the first helper.

The helper shook, stood up, and silently left the room. A number quickly vanished from the control board screen. As he passed Freder, who was now standing near the door, the helper nodded respectfully.

Freder saw the huge clock, which took up one whole wall of the room. Then he saw the wall where the screen continued to flash with numbers. He knew that in this room only the numbers were important.

Joh Fredersen nodded to his helpers to leave the room.

"What do you want, my boy?" he asked without turning around.

"How did you know it was I?" asked Freder softly.

"No one comes to me unannounced, except my son."

"Father, why did you send that man away?" asked Freder.

"Because I have no use for men who make mistakes," said Joh Fredersen, as the numbers danced on the screen.

"But father, perhaps he was ill or . . ."

"Stop feeling sorry for those who suffer," Joh Fredersen interrupted. "If they suffer, it is because they have done something wrong."

"Father, I gained admission to the machine room and I saw suffering people bound to your machine. I saw the faces of men whose children are my brothers and sisters."

"Hmmm," said Joh Fredersen. He began gently tapping a pencil on the table. Seconds of silence flowed between father and son.

Then Freder struck his fists together and shouted, "They are all human beings, **Father**! They live below the ground, and their lives are ruled by the hum of machines."

Joh Fredersen continued the musical tapping of his pencil.

"So, Freder, you think the men are used up by my machines? Well, it is not the fault of the machine. It is the weakness of the human material. Someday I will have an improved man, a machine man."

Freder's tightened fists turned white. He quickly left the room, like a man running to an emergency. In the hall he passed Slim, who had been called to the control room.

Joh Fredersen stood by the window. His eyes wandered over Metropolis, which was now a restless sea, twinkling with waves of light. As always, the hum of the machines was the city's melody.

Joh Fredersen turned slowly and addressed Slim, "From now on I wish to be told of my son's every move."

The man who had been Joh Fredersen's first helper stood in the elevator of the New Tower, his shoulders bent in sadness. The door silently slid open and Freder entered. For a moment the two men stared at each other, seeing in each other's eyes, signs of an emergency.

"What is your name?" Freder asked gently.

The man hesitated and drew in his breath. "Josephat," he said.

"I can help you Josephat," said Freder. "Where do you live?" Josephat's hand fluttered up like a scared bird and he gasped. "Ninety Block, House Seven, Floor Seven," he answered.

"Go there and wait," said Freder. "I will come or send someone who will bring you to me."

Freder began to make his way to the machine room. At the same time, Slim entered Freder's home to question the servants about their master. And while the servants were saying their master was not yet home, Freder was entering the room from which Metropolis got her energy. There was not one human sound in the room. It sounded like a concert of machines. There was a melody of whirring and

clumping, and a musical rumbling ran through the floor and walls. In the middle of the room crouched a huge machine whose limbs shone with oil. Its limbs moved back and forth, and out of its pipes came boiling air.

At the machine stood a man dressed in the clothes of a worker. He held his hand to the lever of the machine and kept his eyes on the clock above. A cloud of hot steam swirled around him and suddenly he fell. Freder caught him as the clouds of steam surrounded them like fog.

"What is your name?" asked Freder.

"11811," was the man's reply.

"No, I want your real name," smiled Freder.

"Georgi," the man answered weakly. Then Georgi became excited, "My machine!" he cried. "Somebody must watch my machine!"

Freder rested his hand on Georgi's shoulder and said, "We will now exchange lives, Georgi. We will change clothes. You take my life and I will take yours at the machine. There is enough money in my pocket for you to take a car to the Ninetieth Block. Find the Seventh House and go to the Seventh Floor. There lives a man named Josephat. Tell him I sent you and wait for me there."

The son of the Master of Metropolis was standing in front of the machine. He wore the clothes of a worker, held his hand to the lever, and kept his eyes on the clock above. Clouds of steam and oil swirled around him. Pulling a rag from his pocket to wipe the sweat from his face, he found a torn piece of paper. It looked like a map, and in the center were a group of crosses.

Meanwhile, Georgi stood in the night air listening to the musical sounds of the city. He reached into his pocket and felt the money. Georgi looked at the city's blocks of lights. Such excitement! There were shows, concerts! Again Georgi felt the money in his pocket. That money would be his admission to the life of the city. He took a car, but he did not go to the Ninetieth Block.

15

Freder's Decision

COMPREHENSION CHECK

Choose the best answer.

1. Joh Fredersen sent the first helper away because
    _____ a. he felt sorry for him.
    _____ b. he had no use for a man who made mistakes.
    _____ c. the helper was ill.
    _____ d. he had too many helpers near the control board.

2. Some day, Joh Fredersen hoped to have
    _____ a. machine men.
    _____ b. a lot of money.
    _____ c. more men like Josephat.
    _____ d. peace and quiet.

3. Joh Fredersen wanted Slim to tell him
    _____ a. where Josephat lived.
    _____ b. his real name.
    _____ c. everything Freder did.
    _____ d. how Freder got into the machine room.

4. First, Freder spoke with his father. Then, he spoke to Josephat in the elevator. Next,
    _____ a. he changed clothes with Josephat.
    _____ b. he ran from the room.
    _____ c. he caught Georgi as he fell.
    _____ d. he told Josephat to go home and wait.

5. Freder was different from his father because
    _____ a. Freder cared about the workers.
    _____ b. Freder was easily frightened.
    _____ c. Freder liked music.
    _____ d. Freder loved the machines.

6. Freder met Georgi
    _____ a. at the control board.
    _____ b. in the machine room.
    _____ c. in the street.
    _____ d. at a show in the city.

7. In the pocket of Georgi's clothes, Freder found
    _____ a. a piece of paper that looked like a map.
    _____ b. a lot of money.
    _____ c. a piece of paper with Josephat's address.
    _____ d. a part from a machine.

8. Georgi didn't go to the Ninetieth Block because
    _____ a. he didn't know the way.
    _____ b. he didn't have enough money.
    _____ c. he was afraid of Freder.
    _____ d. he wanted to enjoy the city.

9. Another name for this story could be
    _____ a. "Freder Chooses a New Life."
    _____ b. "Georgi Becomes a Worker."
    _____ c. "Machine Men in Metropolis."
    _____ d. "The Ninety Block."

10. This story is mainly about
    _____ a. how and why Freder decides to trade lives with Georgi.
    _____ b. how cruel Joh Fredersen is.
    _____ c. how Josephat made a mistake at the control board.
    _____ d. the best way to run a machine.

Check your answers with the key on page 67.

Freder's Decision

VOCABULARY CHECK

admission	concert	emergency	hum	melody	musical

I. Sentences to Finish

Fill in the blank in each sentence with the correct key word from the box above.

1. It is important to stay calm in an _____ .

2. Susan's sweet and _____ voice could be heard above the others.

3. The school band is giving a _____ tonight.

4. We are showing a movie and charging each person fifty cents _____ .

5. Happy people often sing or _____ as they work.

6. All day long Mike whistled the _____ he had heard that morning.

II. Hidden Word

Write the key word that fits each definition in the spaces. Unscramble the circled letters to find another name for Freder's father.

1. anything to do with music

2. a sound made with lips closed

3. a time of sudden trouble

4. performance of musician or musicians

5. the price you pay to be let in

6. a song or tune

1. __ __ __ __ _Ⓞ_ __

2. __ __Ⓞ__

3. __ __ __Ⓞ__ __ __ __ __

4. __ __ __ __ __ _Ⓞ_

5. __ __ __ __ __Ⓞ__ __

6. __Ⓞ__ __ __ __

Another name for Freder's father is _____ .

Check your answers with the key on page 69.

A Strange Visit

PREPARATION

Key Words

bough	(bou)	a branch of a tree *The leaves on the bough were turning green.*
crush	(krush)	to press down hard *Please do not crush the pillow.*
dense	(dens)	packed thickly together *The fog was so dense we could not see.*
flung	(flung)	threw with force *He flung the basketball against the backboard.*
monster	(mon´ stər)	any animal or plant that is frightening because it is unusual *Some people think there is a monster in the lake.*
timber	(tim´ bər)	a number of trees growing in the woods *In a forest fire, much timber can be destroyed.*

A Strange Visit

Necessary Words

crystal   (kris´ tl)   a clear piece of glass that looks like ice
She wore a bracelet that shone like <u>crystal</u>.

sway   (swā)   to swing back and forth; rock from side to side
The water and wind caused the anchored boats to <u>sway</u>.

People

Rotwang   is a scientist and inventor who works for Joh Fredersen.

Hel   was the love of Rotwang the inventor before she became Joh Fredersen's wife and Freder's mother.

Places

City of the Dead   is the original city that stood where Metropolis now stands. It is buried far beneath Metropolis and has a system of tunnels where its dead are buried.

Things

Futura   is a "woman" creature being created by Rotwang in answer to Joh Fredersen's request for machine men.

A Strange Visit

A creature of metal and glass stood near the table in Rotwang's house, as Rotwang and Joh Fredersen examined a map of the City of the Dead.

Preview:
1. Read the name of the story.
2. Look at the picture.
3. Read the sentence under the picture.
4. Read the first paragraph of the story.
5. Then answer the following question.

You learned from your preview that
_____ a. a wicked magician lived in Joh Fredersen's Metropolis.
_____ b. there was a mysterious old house in Metropolis.
_____ c. Metropolis was not a good place to live.
_____ d. a strange, old house was torn down.

Turn to the Comprehension Check on page 22 for the right answer.

Now read the story.

Read to find out more about Rotwang and the creature.

A Strange Visit

Tucked between the towering buildings of Metropolis was an old house. It was even older than the church. For hundreds of years, strange tales surrounded the house. Some said a wicked magician built it, but no one knew for sure. Finally, there came a day when the people said it must be torn down. But the house was stronger than their words, as it was stronger than the years. With suddenly falling stones, the house would crush anyone who tried to tear it down. Others who came near the house died, and no doctor knew the sickness. So strongly did the house fight being destroyed, that people stayed away from it. Soon the little town around the house became a large town. Then the timber gave way to a city, and the city grew into Metropolis, and Metropolis became the center of the world.

One day a man came from far away and said, "I want that house!" He bought it for a very low price, and moved in. This man was a scientist called Rotwang. Few knew him and many stayed away from him. Only Joh Fredersen knew him well, for Joh Fredersen depended upon the inventions of Rotwang to run the machine city of Metropolis.

On the same night that Freder was at the machine, Joh Fredersen was at the door of Rotwang's house. It was hard for him to go to Rotwang, for there was a deep hate between the two men. Both had loved the same woman, but Joh Fredersen married her, and she died soon after Freder was born. Rotwang never forgave Joh Fredersen. In this great love and in this great hate, the woman, Hel, remained alive to both men.

Joh Fredersen silently entered the darkness of Rotwang's house. Out of the dense shadows came a voice, "You must wait a little while longer, Joh Fredersen."

"Listen, Rotwang," said Fredersen, "you know I come to you when I need something. You are the only man who can say that about himself, but I have little time to waste!"

The far-off voice laughed and Joh Fredersen tightened his fists in anger. He screamed at Rotwang, "I would crush your head if only it did not contain such an important brain!"

The far-off voice laughed again. "There is nothing more you can do to me, Joh Fredersen. Which thing do you think is more painful: to smash the head or tear out the heart? You took Hel away from me. That cost me my heart."

Joh Fredersen turned in disgust and walked to a table. He flung aside some books and papers and sat down. He took a piece of paper from his pocket and studied it. It looked like a map and had lines from all directions that led to a place filled with crosses.

Suddenly, he felt something cold on his shoulder. Joh Fredersen turned to see a slender, bony hand grasping him. He could see right through the tightly stretched skin that covered its thin bones. The snow-white hand reached down and took the map from the table.

Startled, Joh Fredersen swung completely around and what he saw looked like some sort of monster! Before him stood a woman whose body was swaying back and forth like the bough of a young tree in the wind. The body looked like crystal and the bones shone like silver. It had no face; only a lump of clay at the end of its neck.

"Be nice, my beauty," said the far-off voice from the dense shadows. "Greet Joh Fredersen, Master of the great Metropolis."

The being bent forward as Joh Fredersen flung out his hands to push it away. Rotwang suddenly appeared. He was a short man with wild, gray hair and deep blue eyes that glowed like a fire when the wind blows through the flames.

"What is that monster?" demanded Joh Fredersen.

"Not what, but who?" replied Rotwang. "It is Futura. But she is not yet finished, for she must have a face. You must give her that because you were the one who ordered her."

"I ordered machine men, not women!" screamed **Fredersen.**

Rotwang smiled. "She can do anything because I have given her special powers. I will make her beautiful, then send her among your enemies, the Gothics, and they will kneel before her. Through her, you can destroy them."

"If she is so special," replied Fredersen, "ask her what the marks on that map mean."

Rotwang smiled again as he looked at the map. "You are at that place," he said. "This house has a door which leads to the stairs that go down to the tunnels beneath Metropolis. It is called the City of the Dead. Years ago, when there was timber all around, there was another town. Metropolis now stands over the remains of that town."

"Why then do the workers want a map to that town?"

"Ah," laughed Rotwang. "Come back tonight dressed as a worker, and I will show you."

"Very well," said Joh Fredersen as he turned to leave.

The being glided up to him and stretched out an arm that was as slender as a bough. It spread open its palm, like a crystal fan, to shake hands. Putting his hand in its palm, Joh Fredersen felt like he had been burned by its coldness.

"Good-by," said the clay head. "Please give me my face soon."

When Joh Fredersen reached the New Tower, Slim was waiting for him. "I must tell you, Mr. Fredersen, that your son is missing!"

"What!" cried Joh Fredersen. "Find him! For what do I pay you? Find him!"

A Strange Visit

COMPREHENSION CHECK

Choose the best answer.

1. Joh Fredersen and Rotwang hated each other because
    _____ a. they had both loved the same woman.
    _____ b. Rotwang tried to help the workers.
    _____ c. Rotwang had captured Freder.
    _____ d. one was good and the other was evil.

2. First, Joh Fredersen entered the house. Then, he spoke with Rotwang. Next,
    _____ a. he took a piece of paper from his pocket.
    _____ b. he sat down at a table.
    _____ c. a slender hand grasped him.
    _____ d. Rotwang appeared.

3. Joh Fredersen took from his pocket
    _____ a. something that looked like a map.
    _____ b. money to pay Rotwang.
    _____ c. a note from Slim.
    _____ d. a picture of a monster.

4. The hand Joh Fredersen felt on his shoulder belonged to
    _____ a. a woman with no face.
    _____ b. Rotwang.
    _____ c. his wife, Hel.
    _____ d. one of the workers.

5. Rotwang said Futura would destroy
    _____ a. Joh Fredersen's son.
    _____ b. the city.
    _____ c. Joh Fredersen's enemies.
    _____ d. the world.

6. Rotwang is best described as
    _____ a. a clever scientist.
    _____ b. an evil scientist.
    _____ c. Joh Fredersen's only friend.
    _____ d. Joh Fredersen's only enemy.

7. Rotwang told Joh Fredersen to come back
    _____ a. when he found Freder.
    _____ b. with a map.
    _____ c. in a few days.
    _____ d. dressed as a worker.

8. When Joh Fredersen shook Futura's hand, he felt like he had been
    _____ a. burned by its coldness.
    _____ b. burned by its heat.
    _____ c. lucky to meet her.
    _____ d. stung by a bee.

9. Another name for this story could be
    _____ a. "Falling Stones."
    _____ b. "The Enemies."
    _____ c. "In Rotwang's House."
    _____ d. "Futura's Brain."

10. This story is mainly about
    _____ a. how Joh Fredersen meets Futura.
    _____ b. Freder's disappearance.
    _____ c. how the old house kept people away.
    _____ d. Rotwang's plan to destroy Metropolis.

Check your answers with the key on page 67.

A Strange Visit

VOCABULARY CHECK

bough	crush	dense	flung	monster	timber

I. Sentences to Finish

Fill in the blank in each sentence with the correct key word from the box above.

1. The man _____ his hat to the ground in anger.

2. The storm tore a _____ from the big oak tree.

3. Jim worked hard to clear away the _____ weeds.

4. The men cut just enough _____ to give them wood for the winter.

5. If you run through the garden, you will _____ the flowers.

6. The baby thinks her sister is really a _____ when she makes that scary face.

II. Making Sense of Sentences

Are the statements below true or false? Place a check next to the correct answer.

1. When Tom <u>flung</u> out his arms, he moved them slowly. _____ True _____ False

2. To <u>crush</u> something is to press down hard on it. _____ True _____ False

3. Another name for many trees growing in the woods is <u>timber</u>. _____ True _____ False

4. A <u>bough</u> is a tool used to cut down trees. _____ True _____ False

5. In a <u>dense</u> forest, there are huge spaces between the trees. _____ True _____ False

6. There might be a <u>monster</u> in a scary movie. _____ True _____ False

Check your answers with the key on page 69.

The City of the Dead

PREPARATION

Key Words

aisle	(īl)	an open space between rows of chairs *She walked down the aisle to the back of the classroom.*
invisible	(in viz′ ə bəl)	not able to be seen *The magician waved his wand and suddenly the rabbit was invisible.*
mask	(mask)	a cover for the face *Jenny wore a white sheet and a scary mask on Halloween.*
pal	(pal)	friend *John has been Stuart's pal since the first grade.*
recess	(rē′ ses, ri ses′)	a short time away from work or school *Everyone was glad when it was time for recess.*
sturdy	(ster′ dē)	strong *Margie was sturdy enough to carry an armload of wood into the house.*

The City of the Dead

Necessary Words

mass   (mas)   a piece or amount of anything without any clear shape or size
The baker's hands were a mass of dough as he prepared the bread.

hissed   (hist)   made a sound like "ss"
The steam hissed as it escaped from the pot of boiling water.

desperate   driven to take any risk; nearly hopeless
John was desperate to find his lost dog.

dismissed   (dis mist´)   sent away
We dismissed the painter because his work was so poor.

People

Maria   is the young woman who leads the workers of Metropolis. Earlier in the story, she appeared in the Eternal Gardens of the Club of the Sons leading the workers' children to see Freder and their "brothers in white silk".

The City of the Dead

Wearing the clothes of a worker, Freder made a promise to Maria in the underground City of the Dead. Rotwang and Joh Fredersen listened and watched from their hiding place.

Preview:
1. Read the name of the story.
2. Look at the picture.
3. Read the sentences under the picture.
4. Read the first three paragraphs of the story.
5. Then answer the following question.

You learned from your preview that
_____ a. Joh Fredersen called to Freder.
_____ b. Freder enjoyed being a worker.
_____ c. Freder wanted to learn more about the workers.
_____ d. Joh Fredersen wanted to learn more about the workers.

Turn to the Comprehension Check on page 28 for the right answer.

Now read the story.

Read to find out what happens in the City of the Dead.

The City of the Dead

Joh Fredersen did not know that his son, Freder, was standing in front of one of the man-eating machines. He could not see that Freder was no longer a sturdy man, but only a dripping mass of sweat. He could not hear his son as he cried, "Oh, Father! Is there no end? Your machines roar on with no recess for the suffering men."

Once more, it was time. Joh Fredersen pressed his fingers to the control board, and the roar of the machines stopped. A recess at last! Freder's head dropped to his chest, and he fell to the floor.

Suddenly, he heard the voice of a man. "She has called. Are you coming?" the man whispered. Freder did not know what the question meant, but he nodded. He wanted to learn the ways of those who wore dark clothes and hard shoes.

It seemed to Freder that he was being led to the center of the earth. Deeper and still deeper down into the folds of darkness they went. Here and there he saw the light of candles held in men's hands. "We must be in a tunnel," Freder thought.

At last they came to a wide, lit area. Hundreds of workers sat in rows. Each one held a candle. In front of the workers stood a beautiful woman, the same woman Freder had seen in The Club of the Sons! Freder began to walk up the aisle toward the woman as if pulled by an invisible hand.

"My brothers," the woman said, "you are the hands that run the machine city, and the New Tower is the brain. The hands and the brain should always work together. But now they have become enemies and someone must make peace between them. There are many of you who say fight, but I say wait. Someone will come to help us. Be patient, my brothers."

A murmur ran through the rows of men. "We shall wait, Maria, but not much longer," they said.

The workers filed silently out and Freder was left standing alone in front of Maria.

"I shall be the one to help you," he said.

"Why does the son of Joh Fredersen wear the clothes of a worker?" asked the young woman. "Why do you come beneath the earth where there is no rain, sun or moon? Do you come to the City of the Dead only to make fun of us?"

"Have you no faith in me?" asked Freder. "I shall always wear these clothes, but not as Joh Fredersen's son. Joh Frederson no longer has a son!"

Meanwhile, invisible to Maria and Freder, Joh Fredersen and Rotwang stood in a tunnel, listening.

"You wanted me to give Futura a face," hissed Joh Fredersen. "Well there it is. Give her a face just like Maria's, and do it quickly!"

Freder and Maria parted with promises to meet again. Maria made her way back through the dark tunnels, unaware that she was being followed. She smiled as she thought about her love for Freder.

Maria stopped suddenly at the whisper of her name. She wondered if Freder had come back. She called to him, but there was no answer. Then a strange coldness settled upon her and there came a sigh that would not end.

She saw a gliding figure at the end of the tunnel and she was sure it was no pal. Maria put out her light and slipped into a second tunnel. There she waited for the feet to pass, but the feet stopped in front of where she hid.

She felt her way through the tunnel as the sound of her own heartbeat grew louder in her ears. Soon, the tunnel was lit by a pale glow. And the glow came from the figure's jellyfish head. At first Maria thought is was a mask, but she soon realized it was a formless lump.

The being stretched out a slender, glowing arm toward her. Screaming, Maria ran down the tunnel and came upon old, stone stairs. The stairs led to a sturdy stone door. She pushed her head and shoulders against the door. It fell back with a crash, and she swung herself over the edge. She opened an unlocked door and found herself in a gloomy old house. It was Rotwang's house!

Rotwang came toward her. The shadows fell so darkly across his face that he looked as though he was wearing a mask. As Rotwang reached out toward her, Maria gasped and the room faded to darkness.

Meanwhile, Slim continued his search for Freder in the sparkling city of Metropolis. He sought out Freder's pals in the clubs and theaters, but they did not know where he could be found. Desperate, Slim entered a night club. As he walked down the aisle, he saw that a drunk man was causing a problem.

The club owner shrugged his shoulders in disgust. "That man wears the white silks that are made for only a special few in Metropolis. But he thinks he's a machine."

Slim recognized the drunk man as Georgi from the machine room of Metropolis. Georgi was waving his hands wildly in the air and shouting, "I am death. I am a machine!"

Slim caught Georgi just as he fell and brought him to a doctor.

Slim bent over the man in the torn white silk. "How did you get the white silk clothes, Georgi?"

A voice answered, softer than a whisper. "Freder, Joh Fredersen's son, changed with me and told me I was to wait for him."

"Wait where, Georgi?"

A very long silence hung in the air, then a whisper came through his tears. "Ninetieth Street, House Seven, Seventh Floor," Georgi whispered.

Slim knew who lived there. It was Josephat, the man who had been dismissed by Joh Fredersen. Slim quickly turned and left the room. He paused outside, drew in a deep breath of the night air, and took a car to Ninetieth Street.

The City of the Dead

COMPREHENSION CHECK

Choose the best answer.

1. Freder followed the man from the machine room into
    _____ a. Rotwang's house.
    _____ b. the New Tower.
    _____ c. a Tunnel.
    _____ d. a night club.

2. In front of the workers, stood
    _____ a. Futura.
    _____ b. Freder.
    _____ c. the woman Freder had seen in the Club of the Sons.
    _____ d. a strange being with a jellyfish head.

3. Maria told the workers they should
    _____ a. fight.
    _____ b. wait and be patient.
    _____ c. leave her alone.
    _____ d. have faith in Freder.

4. Freder said Joh Fredersen no longer had a son because
    _____ a. Freder had forgotten who he was.
    _____ b. Freder was planning to run away to another city.
    _____ c. Freder was trying to trick Maria.
    _____ d. Freder didn't believe in the same things his father did.

5. Joh Fredersen told Rotwang to give Futura
    _____ a. a face that glowed in the dark.
    _____ b. a face just like Maria's.
    _____ c. a candle for the dark.
    _____ d. a mask to cover her face.

6. First, Maria heard a whisper. Then, she saw a figure in the tunnel. Next,
    _____ a. the tunnel was lit by a glow.
    _____ b. Freder stood alone in front of Maria.
    _____ c. Rotwang reached out for Maria.
    _____ d. Maria ran screaming down the tunnel.

7. When Maria ran up the stairs and through the door, she found herself
    _____ a. in a wide lit area.
    _____ b. in the City of the Dead.
    _____ c. in Rotwang's house.
    _____ d. outside in the dark.

8. After finding Georgi, Slim headed for
    _____ a. Rotwang's house.
    _____ b. Josephat's house.
    _____ c. Joh Fredersen's house.
    _____ d. Georgi's house.

9. Another name for this story could be
    _____ a. "Georgi's Mistake."
    _____ b. "Freder in Danger."
    _____ c. "Beneath the City."
    _____ d. "The Man-Eating Machines."

10. This story is mainly about
    _____ a. how Freder worked at the machine.
    _____ b. Slim's search for Freder.
    _____ c. how Georgi caused a disturbance.
    _____ d. Maria and the workers.

Check your answers with the key on page 67.

The City of the Dead

VOCABULARY CHECK

aisle	invisible	mask	pal	recess	sturdy

I. Sentences to Finish

Fill in the blank in each sentence with the correct key word from the box above.

1. Rob became my _____ when we worked together at the school fair.

2. The chair didn't look _____ enough to sit on.

3. Ruthie spilled her popcorn in the _____ of the theater.

4. The class couldn't go outdoors for _____ because of the rain.

5. The bird was so well hidden that it was almost _____ .

6. The robber wore a _____ so no one would recognize him.

II. Crossword Puzzle

Fill in the puzzle with the key word from the box above. Use the meanings below to help you choose the right word.

Across

2. strong

4. friend

6. not able to be seen

Down

1. a cover for the face

3. a short time away from school or work

5. an open space between rows of chairs

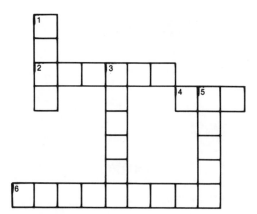

Check your answers with the key on page 70.

This page may be reproduced for classroom use.

Fighting Against A Dreadful Power

PREPARATION

Key Words

clutch	(kluch)	hold on to tightly *If the man does not <u>clutch</u> the box of food, the dog will get it away from him.*
dodge	(doj)	move quickly to one side to avoid something; avoid *She tried to <u>dodge</u> the crowd on the sidewalk.*
hasty	(hā´ stē)	fast; rushed done without thinking *Mother told Susan not to make a <u>hasty</u> decision about which dress to buy.*
junk	(jungk)	old rags, metal, or other material no longer of worth *Old cars often are taken to the <u>junk</u> yard.*
pace	(pās)	1. a step *When John was late, Sue began to <u>pace</u> around the room.* 2. speed; how fast someone or something moves *Race horses gallop at a very fast <u>pace</u>.*
value	(val´ yu̇)	having worth; importance *Wood has great <u>value</u> to a carpenter.*

Fighting Against A Dreadful Power

Necessary Words

horror	(hôr′ ər)	something very bad or unpleasant; scarey

The boy watched in <u>horror</u> as the dog stepped out into the busy street.

Fighting Against A Dreadful Power

Slim, Freder's guard, tried to make Josephat tell him where Freder was. Freder was searching for Maria, when he saw her face in Rotwang's window.

Preview:
1. Read the name of the story.
2. Look at the picture.
3. Read the sentences under the picture.
4. Read the first three paragraphs of the story.
5. Then answer the following question.

You learned from your preview that
_____ a. Freder was upset that Georgi had not come.
_____ b. Freder was glad that Georgi had not come.
_____ c. Josephat didn't know if Georgi had ever come.
_____ d. Josephat was not telling Freder the truth.

Turn to the Comprehension Check on page 34 for the right answer.

Now read the story.

Read to find out if Josephat, Freder and Maria will get away.

Fighting Against A Dreadful Power

Freder looked around at the three beautiful rooms that were Josephat's home. "Where is Georgi?" he asked in a hasty manner.

"No one has come," answered Josephat in a tired voice. His thin, white face showed the hours he had spent in worry, waiting for Freder. "I sat all night in this chair," continued Josephat. "I did not sleep a wink and nobody has come, Mr. Freder."

Freder remained silent. He raised his hands to clutch at his face, as if he felt some pain there.

"Mr. Freder," Josephat began again, "why are you wearing those clothes?"

"Georgi wore them. I gave him mine. I found him in front of the machine. I took his place and I sent him to you," said Freder.

Josephat sighed and nodded his head. "I now understand why Georgi has not come."

Freder gave him a questioning look, but said nothing.

"No doubt there was money in the clothes you exchanged with Georgi," Josephat said. "Money to be spent on the sparkling delights of Metropolis."

Freder began to pace around the room. "I'm sure Slim is on my trail and he is a difficult man to dodge. He has probably located Georgi, and he will persuade Georgi to tell him where we were to meet. He must not find me, for I am no longer Joh Fredersen's son! Since the same things no longer have value for my father and me, I have set myself free."

Freder looked down at Georgi's black cap that lay on the floor and said further, "I need a friend I can trust. Will you be that friend Josephat?"

Josephat smiled. "Yes, Mr. Freder, I will."

"I must go now, Josephat," Freder said, "for I want to visit my father's mother and bring her something which is of great value. Wait, I will be back soon." The two men clutched each other's hands, then Freder left hastily.

A little later a knock came at the door, and although the knock was gentle, there was something in it that sent a shiver down Josephat's back. The knocking came again and Josephat remained still, looking at the door.

Then the door opened and in walked Slim. He glanced quickly around the room, and his eyes came to rest on the black cap that lay on the floor.

"Where is Freder, Josephat?" Slim asked in a low but firm voice.

"I do not know," replied Josephat, weakly, "and if I did, you could not get it out of me!"

The corner of Slim's mouth curved in a sneaky half-smile. "You are quite right," he said. "It was a stupid question."

Josephat's throat dried up and he dared not move from where he stood.

"I see you live quite well here," said Slim. "You have nice things; no junk. It is too bad you will be leaving soon."

Slim plunged his hands into his pockets and drew out a large pile of money which he placed on a table before Josephat. Then Slim slipped the black cap into his pocket. Josephat's anger blinded him and he looked at the money as if it were junk. Slim sighed and placed a second pile of money on the table.

"I trust," he said flatly, "that this is enough for you to leave Metropolis and start a new life."

"I will not!" shouted Josephat, shaking from head to foot.

Slim shook his head slowly as he placed a third pile of money near the other two. "There is even a plane waiting for you. Is it enough now?"

"Yes," muttered Josephat, "it is enough!" Josephat stared at the black cap that had fallen from Slim's pocket. Then a howl escaped Josephat's lips. He picked up the cap and ran to the door, but Slim got there before him. Josephat stepped aside to dodge Slim, but Slim grabbed him and they began to fight.

The two men pushed and stumbled. They stamped like horses and struck at each other like bears, but, against Slim's steel coldness, Josephat could not hold his ground. Suddenly, as though his legs had been crushed, he fell into Slim's arms.

"I'm sorry," said Slim, cooly, "but you forced me to do it. Are you ready to go now?"

"Yes," said Josephat, weakly. And he took the money Slim handed him.

Josephat walked to the door, picked up the cap Freder had been wearing, and waved it as a good-bye to the room. Then he left and Slim followed him.

Freder paced through the shadows of the dark church where he was to meet Maria, but she was not there. Finally, worn out with sadness, Freder left to wander through the streets of Metropolis. He soon came upon the old house which could not be destroyed. It was Rotwang's house.

Through the hum of the machine city, Freder thought he heard a thin voice cry for help. Freder stopped. He could not believe what he saw. Maria's face appeared through one of the windows of the old house. Freder banged on the door, but the only answer was the silent gloom. When he went to throw himself against the door, it quietly opened. As Freder felt his way in the darkness, the voice of Maria called to him from the heart of the house.

Finally, he reached the stairs and from the top of the stairs came a voice that was as soft and tender as a kiss. "Come. I am here, dearest," it said.

It sounded like Maria's voice, but Freder felt there was something strange about it. The voice begged him, "Look for me!"

He heard soft laughter. Then, through the soft laughter, came another voice. It, too, sounded like Maria, but this voice was sick with fear and filled with horror. "Freder, help me! I do not know what is being done to me!" it cried.

Fighting Against A Dreadful Power

COMPREHENSION CHECK

Choose the best answer.

1. Freder asked Josephat to
    _____ a. give him money.
    _____ b. be his friend.
    _____ c. tell him where Slim was.
    _____ d. come with him.

2. Freder told Josephat he was going
    _____ a. to find his father.
    _____ b. to find Maria.
    _____ c. to leave the city forever.
    _____ d. to visit his father's mother.

3. Slim gave Josephat money
    _____ a. to get him to leave Metropolis.
    _____ b. to pay him for his work.
    _____ c. to pay for the black cap he took.
    _____ d. because the money belonged to Josephat.

4. Josephat agreed to go with Slim because
    _____ a. he wanted the money.
    _____ b. Slim was too strong for him.
    _____ c. he decided to be Slim's friend.
    _____ d. Freder told him to.

5. Freder went to the church
    _____ a. to wait for Josephat.
    _____ b. to meet Maria.
    _____ c. to find Georgi.
    _____ d. to rescue Maria.

6. First, Freder heard a cry for help. Then, he saw Maria's face in the window. Next,
    _____ a. Freder ran to get help.
    _____ b. Freder went into the house.
    _____ c. Freder disappeared.
    _____ d. Freder banged on the door.

7. The voice of Maria came from
    _____ a. Josephat's house.
    _____ b. the City of the Dead.
    _____ c. Rotwang's house.
    _____ d. the old church.

8. Freder thought it sounded as though Maria
    _____ a. was glad to see him.
    _____ b. had two different voices.
    _____ c. was far, far away.
    _____ d. was laughing at him.

9. Another name for this story could be
    _____ a. "Trouble for Friends and Lovers."
    _____ b. "Josephat's New Job."
    _____ c. "Georgi Returns."
    _____ d. "The Meeting at the Church."

10. This story is mainly about
    _____ a. how Rotwang's house becomes a meeting place for Slim and his friends.
    _____ b. the great changes that are taking place in the lives of the characters.
    _____ c. how Freder decides to return to his old way of life and forget Maria.
    _____ d. the honest way that Joh Fredersen guides the people of Metropolis.

Check your answers with the key on page 67.

This page may be reproduced for classroom use.

Fighting Against A Dreadful Power

VOCABULARY CHECK

clutch	dodge	hasty	junk	pace	value

I. Sentences to Finish

Fill in the blank in each sentence with the correct key word from the box above.

1. Lucy gasped when the man told her the _____ of her jewels.

2. Peter had to _____ the umbrella to keep it from blowing away.

3. A pile of _____ by the side of the road spoiled the beautiful view.

4. People who are worried sometimes _____ around the room.

5. Karen wrote a _____ note and ran out the door.

6. The morning after the first snow, Tom had to _____ snowballs all the way to school.

II. Word Search

All the words from the box above are hidden in the puzzle below. Find each word and draw a circle around it.

```
A M H T P O J K D O
G P A V A L U E O H
N E R U C H N A C E
D O D G E A K J L U
T U V A N L E G U A
O J U E T H A S T Y
C E D O G N U E C L
V A U H O D C S H T
```

Check your answers with the key on page 70.

Difficult Times

PREPARATION

Key Words

alter   (ôl´ tər)   to change in size or style
My sister wanted to <u>alter</u> her dress by making it longer.

appreciate   (ə prē´shē āt)   to think highly of
Everyone will <u>appreciate</u> your kindness.

capital   (cap´ ə təl)   the city where a state or nation has its main government offices
The <u>capital</u> of Wisconsin is Madison.

garment   (g̈ar´ mənt)   a piece of clothing
A raincoat is a <u>garment</u> for bad weather.

geography   (jē og´ rə fē)   the study of the earth and its life
In <u>geography</u>, you learn about all the nations of the world.

spaghetti   (spə get´ ē)   a food made of flour and water
My favorite meal is <u>spaghetti</u> with meat sauce.

Difficult Times

Necessary Words

haste   (hāst)   trying to be quick; hurrying
> *In her haste to finish the assignment, the student made some careless mistakes.*

Difficult Times

Maria sat very still in one room of Rotwang's house. In the next room, Rotwang formed the creature that would look and sound just like Maria.

Preview:
1. Read the name of the story.
2. Look at the picture.
3. Read the sentences under the picture.
4. Read the first three paragraphs of the story.
5. Then answer the following question.

You learned from your preview that
_____ a. Maria had escaped from Rotwang's house.
_____ b. Maria no longer loved Freder.
_____ c. Rotwang had taken Maria away.
_____ d. Rotwang was keeping Maria in his house.

Turn to the Comprehension Check on page 40 for the right answer.

Now read the story.

Read to find out more about Rotwang's plan for the creature.

Difficult Times

Freder ran down the hall like a blind animal. He banged on doors of empty rooms, ran around corners, and stumbled up stairs. But he was running in circles, always covering his own steps. He heard the sweetly wicked voice singing, "Look for me, my love. I am here!"

Freder stumbled and fell. He tried to get up, but a blanket of darkness settled upon him and he went into a deep sleep.

Rotwang saw Freder fall. When he was sure that Freder was perfectly still, the great inventor came out of hiding. He opened one of the doors and entered a room to find Maria as he always found her, sitting stiffly in a high, narrow chair in a far corner of the room.

"Won't you smile and cry just once, Maria?" asked Rotwang, the inventor. "I need your smile and your tears or you will destroy my work."

The girl stared over and beyond him.

"You two children have dared to go against Joh Fredersen, but he will not allow his son to be taken from him. Do you believe Freder loves you?"

Maria remained still, but around her rosebud mouth a smile began to blossom.

"Joh Fredersen does not appreciate your love for his son," said Rotwang. "Freder will have forgotten you by the day he gets married."

"Never!" screamed Maria, as tears fell upon the beauty of her smile.

Rotwang went into the next room and stared at the being he had made from glass and metal. It had the almost-completed head of Maria. The shining being looked at Rotwang with cool eyes, and its mysterious laughter filled the air.

When Freder awoke, he found himself surrounded by a dull light that was coming through a small window. He pulled himself up, and through the window he saw Maria walking down in the street. He cried her name, but she continued her hasty step.

To the sound of his boiling blood, Freder beat against the door until it broke. He ran after Maria, but the sea of people had washed her away. Then Freder heard the New Tower roar like the sea and howl like a storm.

"My father!" Freder thought. "I will go to my father and ask him what Rotwang has done to Maria."

When Freder reached the New Tower, he ran up to his father's office and pushed open the door. What he saw turned him to stone, for Joh Fredersen was holding Maria in his arms. Freder began to push his father out of the way. He saw his father only as a living wall between himself and his Maria. The creature that looked like Maria watched silently; a smile played around the corners of her mouth.

Suddenly, Freder's legs felt as soft as spaghetti and he fell to the floor. "Where is Maria?" he cried.

"No one has been here," Joh Fredersen said calmly. "You are ill, my son."

Meanwhile, the plane that took Josephat away from the machine capital of Metropolis flew in the golden air of the setting sun. The plane was rising and falling. Inside the plane, Josephat was fighting with the pilot to turn back.

But the pilot would not alter the plane's direction. The plane continued moving through the sky, and soon a silver-gray cloth dropped from it and puffed out like a cloud. Pushed and pulled by the wind, it swung back and forth, fluttering down to earth.

Josephat freed himself from the parachute's tangled spaghetti-like cords. He lay still for awhile, his eyes searching the sky. He saw the plane rushing madly toward the setting sun, and he knew that at the wheel sat a man who would not turn back. The man could not alter the plane's course, for he was dead, killed by Josephat.

Josephat looked around at the open field. He did not know the geography of the countryside,

but he guessed at the direction he would have to walk to return to the machine city and his friend Freder, whom he had deserted. When Josephat reached the city, he tried to see Freder, but there was always a stranger or worker who would not allow him to do so.

Josephat never saw Freder leave the house, but he watched his friend stand near the window. Freder looked out on the machine city, but could no longer appreciate what he saw. He had grown so thin that his silk garment hung loosely around him. Josephat knew all of this. "There must be some way to get up there to see him," thought Josephat.

Freder continued to look out over Metropolis. He studied its geography, which spread before him in twisted streets and glowing towers. A flash of light struck like a match over the city, and the rumbling thunder and heavy rain swallowed up the sound of the door that opened behind him. When Freder turned around, he found Josephat standing in the middle of the room, wearing the garments of a worker.

The men walked toward each other as if driven by a strange power. Freder seized his friend's arm in haste.

"I am sorry," he said. "You waited for me, but I could not send you a message. Please forgive me."

Josephat hung his head. "I have nothing to forgive you, Mr. Freder. I did not wait for you," he said, softly.

Then each man waited to tell the other his story.

Difficult Times

COMPREHENSION CHECK

Choose the best answer.

1. Rotwang wanted Maria to smile and cry because
_____ a. he thought teasing her was funny.
_____ b. he needed her smile and tears to make the creature.
_____ c. her love for Freder made him jealous.
_____ d. Joh Fredersen had ordered him to do so.

2. From glass and metal, Rotwang had made
_____ a. an airplane.
_____ b. a creature that looked like Freder.
_____ c. a creature that looked like Maria.
_____ d. a high, narrow chair.

3. When Freder saw Maria in the street, he
_____ a. smiled.
_____ b. sobbed.
_____ c. broke down the door.
_____ d. watched her silently.

4. The woman that Freder thought was Maria was
_____ a. really Maria, his love.
_____ b. Futura, the creature Rotwang had made.
_____ c. a friend of Maria's.
_____ d. just Freder's imagination.

5. First, Josephat fought with the pilot. Then, Josephat jumped from the plane. Next,
_____ a. he killed the pilot.
_____ b. he walked to the city.
_____ c. he tried to see Freder.
_____ d. he watched Freder at the window.

6. The silver-gray object that dropped from the sky was
_____ a. a plane.
_____ b. a cloud.
_____ c. Josephat's shirt.
_____ d. a parachute.

7. Josephat saw that Freder had
_____ a. grown thin.
_____ b. grown fat.
_____ c. deserted him.
_____ d. forgotten him.

8. Freder and Josephat were
_____ a. angry at each other.
_____ b. glad to see each other.
_____ c. afraid of each other.
_____ d. sorry to see each other.

9. Another name for this story could be
_____ a. "Hard Work."
_____ b. "Unhappy Events."
_____ c. "Making Changes."
_____ d. "Trying Hard."

10. This story is mainly about
_____ a. giving in to an enemy.
_____ b. being kind to others.
_____ c. being selfish.
_____ d. being true to friends.

Check your answers with the key on page 67.

Difficult Times

VOCABULARY CHECK

alter	appreciate	capital	garment	geography	spaghetti

I. Sentences to Finish

Fill in the blank in each sentence with the correct key word from the box above.

1. We visited our state _____ and shook hands with the governor.

2. While eating, Mark spilled _____ sauce on his shirt.

3. That old jacket is Grandfather's favorite _____ .

4. Once the walls were up, it was too late to _____ the plans for the new house.

5. Carol finds _____ interesting because she loves to look at maps and learn about far-off places.

6. Your mother would _____ a gift you made yourself.

II. Hidden Answer

Write in the spaces the key word that fits each definition. The circled letters will tell you the answer to the riddle below.

1. to think highly of

2. a food made of flour and water

3. a piece of clothing

4. city where government offices are

5. to change

6. the study of earth

Riddle: What can you wear every day that never gets too small and never gets worn out?

Answer: ___   ___ ___ ___ ___ ___ (two words)

Check your answers with the key on page 70.

The Dance of Death

PREPARATION

Key Words

chamber   (chām′ bər)   a room
>*They walked into the chamber and closed the door.*

compact   (kəm pakt′)   to make smaller; pack closely together
>*We must compact the laundry so that it will fit into the bag.*

furious   (fyur′ ē əs)   very angry
>*She was furious when her dress was torn.*

peculiar   (pi kyü′ lyər)   strange or unusual
>*The peculiar noises were being made by insects.*

practical   (prak′ tə kəl)   useful
>*I keep only practical items in the kitchen.*

having or showing good sense
>*John was a practical man and he saved some money from his pay each week.*

system   (sis′ təm)   a plan or way of doing things
>*He had a good system for doing math.*

The Dance of Death

Necessary Words

monk   (mungk)   a man who gives up all worldly things and lives with other men to serve God through hard work
The monk had to rise at dawn to begin his many chores.

sin   (sin)   breaking the law of God; wrongdoing of any kind
The minister said that stealing is a sin.

evil   (ē′ vəl)   wicked or bad, causing harm
In some fairy tales, witches cast evil spells on people.

shimmering   (shim′ ər ing)   to shine with a flickering light; to gleam softly
When they turned off the lights, the candles on the birthday cake were shimmering.

presence   (prez′ ns)   in the sight or company of
The children were very excited in the presence of the clown.

People

Desertus   is the monk who leads the group of Gothics against the world of Joh Fredersen.

The Dance of Death

Futura, the creature that looked like Maria, turned the workers against Freder.

Preview:
1. Read the name of the story.
2. Look at the picture.
3. Read the sentence under the picture.
4. Read the first two paragraphs of the story.
5. Then answer the following question.

You learned from your preview that
_____ a. Freder had no friends left.
_____ b. Freder had heard about an evil woman.
_____ c. Freder had found Maria again.
_____ d. Freder wanted to set fire to the city.

Turn to the Comprehension Check on page 46 for the right answer.

Now read the story.

Read to find out if Freder will live to help free the real Maria.

The Dance of Death

Freder and Josephat stood together as friends in Freder's flat. Freder told Josephat about that day in The Club of the Sons and about his Maria. He explained how he had fought with his father over a woman who looked like Maria. He could not compact the fear that he had only imagined all these happenings.

Freder's words began to flow like water from a broken pitcher: "One day I went to the church thinking I might find Maria, but instead, the furious voice of Desertus, the monk, flew from inside like a spear. He said that because Metropolis had sinned, an evil woman would set fire to the city.

"I was surprised to see an old friend of mine from The Club of the Sons there next to me. His face bore a peculiar, empty look. I put my hand on Jan's shoulder and asked him of whom Desertus was speaking. Jan turned and gazed at me with empty eyes. I followed him outside and he told me his story.

"Jan said that one day all the important people in Metropolis had received a short note inviting them to a party. It was most peculiar, but they all thought it was a harmless joke so they went.

"Upon arriving at the house, they were shown to a large chamber by a polite, old man. Once they were inside, it became so silent that they could hear the noises of the street roaring like waves against the walls of the chamber.

"The old man addressed the group and introduced a woman he called his daughter. When the woman appeared on the stairs, all the people in the room turned pale at the sight of her shimmering form. Soon it was as though the air was burning. At the same time, a cutting coldness came from the woman.

"The presence of this woman was enough to kill the love in the hearts of those gathered. She brought hate between husband and wife, and between parent and child. The woman's name was Maria."

Freder fixed his eyes on Josephat and continued. "Jan told me something else. He told me that Maria was seen at two places at the same time. She was seen in the window of Rotwang's house and also seen gliding through the streets of Metropolis!"

Josephat looked at Freder. "Many workers are going down through the compact system of tunnels beneath the city to wait for one called Maria, who they say is as true as gold," said Josephat.

"Yes," said Freder, "and I shall go with them!"

It was dark, and through the window, the glare of the city lights fell on Maria's face. She sat in silence, her eyes closed.

"Will you not speak to me?" said Rotwang, trying not to sound furious. "I still hold you prisoner. It is not my fault, for above me there is a system which forces me to be bad. All I ask is for you to forgive one who must be bad. Ever since Joh Fredersen killed Hel, the woman I love, all the good choked up in me."

Silence was Maria's only reply.

"Be practical, Maria!" cried Rotwang. "I know the workers wait for you beneath the city. They wait, but their disappointment grows. You spoke to them of peace and of one who would help them. But I, the great inventor and magician, stole your face and created another you in a different form. Through this form, a message has been sent to your brothers, calling them to the underground city. The other Maria will speak to them of war and hate.

"Don't you understand? Joh Fredersen does not live by a system of peace. He wants the workers to fight so he can destroy them. Please be practical, Maria. Forgive me and I will go with you to your brothers to warn them."

Rotwang heard her soft weeping and fell upon his knees. Suddenly, he listened and stared. He said in a voice which was almost a scream, "Maria, don't you hear? There is someone else in this room!"

"Yes," said the quiet voice of Joh **Fredersen**, as his hands seized the throat of Rotwang, the great inventor . . .

Beneath the city, Freder stood among the workers. He saw the woman with her shimmering face and blood-red mouth. She spoke in a voice that was full of wicked sweetness.

"My brothers," the voice said, "why do you let the machines eat you like food? Stand the world on its head. Destroy the masters and crush the machines!"

A mighty wave of voices cried out, "Lead us on, Maria!" And the workers rushed forward to follow the woman in her dance of death.

"You are not Maria!" shouted Freder.

The woman pointed a shiny finger. "Look! The son of Joh Fredersen is among you. Kill him!" she screamed.

Freder did not run.

"Dog in white silk!" cried the workers at Freder. Then an arm shot up and a knife flashed. But before the knife could plunge into Freder's heart, a man threw himself as a shield in front of Freder's chest.

The knife ripped open blue cotton and the blue cotton turned red. Freder recognized the man as Georgi, the worker with whom he had first exchanged clothes. Then, like the rush of a thousand wings, the crowd pushed forward. On their shoulders, the woman danced and sang, "We've passed a sentence of death on the machines. Death to the machines!"

The Dance of Death

COMPREHENSION CHECK

Choose the best answer.

1. Jan had told Freder about
   _____ a. his daughter.
   _____ b. Joh Fredersen's plan.
   _____ c. a very strange party.
   _____ d. the tunnels under the city.

2. Jan said that Maria had
   _____ a. been to the church.
   _____ b. run away.
   _____ c. not been seen for a long time.
   _____ d. been seen in two places at once.

3. When Josephat told Freder the workers were going to Maria,
   _____ a. Freder didn't believe him.
   _____ b. Freder sent the workers a message.
   _____ c. Freder decided to go with them.
   _____ d. Freder decided to leave Metropolis.

4. Rotwang said he would go with Maria to warn the workers because
   _____ a. he wanted to trick her into going with him.
   _____ b. he knew Joh Fredersen was listening.
   _____ c. he was sorry now for what he had done.
   _____ d. he knew it was too late anyway.

5. Rotwang asked Maria to
   _____ a. save his life.
   _____ b. forgive him.
   _____ c. forget about Freder.
   _____ d. destroy the machines.

6. The false Maria told the workers to
   _____ a. kill and destroy.
   _____ b. live in peace.
   _____ c. listen to Freder.
   _____ d. go back to work.

7. First, Freder shouted, "You are not Maria!" Then, the woman screamed for the workers to kill him. Next,
   _____ a. Freder ran.
   _____ b. a man threw himself in front of Freder.
   _____ c. the woman danced on their shoulders.
   _____ d. a knife flashed.

8. The man who saved Freder's life was
   _____ a. Rotwang.
   _____ b. Josephat.
   _____ c. Georgi.
   _____ d. Joh Fredersen.

9. Another name for this story could be
   _____ a. "A Good Plan."
   _____ b. "Desertus, the Monk."
   _____ c. "The Evil Woman."
   _____ d. "Maria's Mistake."

10. This story is mainly about
    _____ a. Freder's friend Jan.
    _____ b. the two Marias.
    _____ c. Georgi's courage.
    _____ d. Rotwang's evil ways.

Check your answers with the key on page 67.

The Dance of Death

VOCABULARY CHECK

chamber	compact	furious	peculiar	practical	system

I. Sentences to Finish

Fill in the blank in each sentence with the correct key word from the box above.

1. Bill was _____ at Ted for wrecking his new bike.

2. There was a stone _____ in the castle where prisoners were kept.

3. Since the Wilsons bought a machine to _____ their garbage, they don't need their big garbage can any more.

4. We have a new _____ for fire drills this year.

5. Dancing slippers are not very _____ for climbing mountains.

6. You would probably think it _____ to meet a man who wore a flower pot on his head.

II. Finish the Paragraph

Write in each space the key word that fits.

The woman who looked like Maria spoke to the workers in a (1) _____ beneath the city. None of them noticed the (2) _____ change that had come over her. The Maria they used to know had tried to help them find (3) _____ answers to their problems. She believed in a (4) _____ based on peace and love. But this new Maria spoke to them of hate. She seemed able to (5) _____ a huge amount of anger into just a few words. She made the workers so (6) _____ at Freder that they tried to kill him.

Check your answers with the key on page 71.

The Heart-Machine

PREPARATION

Key Words

bonfire	(bon' fīr)	a large, outdoor fire *Everyone gathered sticks and logs to make the bonfire.*
caravan	(kar' ə van)	a large, closed truck used for travel or living *The caravan was their home as they wandered across the country.* group of merchants, pilgrims, etc. traveling together for safety through difficult or dangerous country *The caravan made its way through the desert and arrived at the city where the merchants would sell their goods at a fair price.*
herb	(ėrb, hėrb)	any plant used for making medicines or flavoring foods *When Mrs. Smith needs an herb, she takes it from her garden.*
jewelry	(jü' əl rē)	a group or set of jewels, usually worth a lot of money *Susie loved jewelry; especially rings and bracelets.*
society	(sə sī' ə tē)	a group of people sharing common interests and habits *Every country in the world has its own special type of society.*
stationary	(stā' sh ə ner ē)	not moving *The Warren family was stationary for five years and then moved to a new house.*

The Heart-Machine

Necessary Words

mob   (mob)   a large number of people; sometimes an angry group
The mob almost knocked down the guards as they pushed through the gates.

dome   (dōm)   a large, rounded, high roof or ceiling
The dome of the church was taller than all the houses nearby.

People

Grot   is the worker who loved and ran the machine that was the heart of the city.

CTR E-8
The Heart-Machine

Futura, the creature, led the mob of workers through the door of the machine room to kill the machines that controlled their lives.

Preview:
1. Read the name of the story.
2. Look at the picture.
3. Read the sentence under the picture.
4. Read the first four paragraphs of the story.
5. Then answer the following question.

You learned from your preview that
_____ a. Freder had to try and save Metropolis.
_____ b. Freder had joined the angry crowd.
_____ c. Georgi hoped Metropolis would be destroyed.
_____ d. Georgi thought only of himself.

Turn to the Comprehension Check on page 52 for the right answer.

Now read the story.

Read to find out what will happen in the machine room of Metropolis.

The Heart-Machine

Under Metropolis, the shouts of the mob turned to a rumbling echo as they twisted their way up the tunnel. Their anger was ready to burst like a volcano over Metropolis. Freder stayed back and held the dying Georgi, who had saved his life.

"You must warn the town," Georgi whispered. "I know a short way out and I will show you."

"No!" said Freder. "You must remain stationary, for your first step will be your death."

Georgi grabbed Freder's arm and led him through tunnel after tunnel. Finally, he stumbled and pointed toward a set of stairs. "I can go no further," he groaned, "but you must go. Hurry!"

Freder let go of Georgi's hand and ran up the stairs until the night of Metropolis covered him like a blanket. He ran toward the New Tower of Babel to see his father.

Meanwhile, Maria remained stationary in the room of Rotwang's house. She would not close her eyes, for she was afraid that a new terror would seize her while she blinked. Some time had passed since Joh Fredersen had dragged Rotwang into the next room, and since then Maria had heard nothing more. But now the voice of Metropolis spread through the house like an angry storm cloud. It did not sound like the machines' usual cry for food. The machines cried, "Danger"!

The machines kept screaming and Maria wondered what danger was threatening Metropolis. Then she recalled Rotwang's words. Someone had been sent among the workers to tell them to destroy Metropolis and its society. Maria ran out of the room, found the trap door which led to the underground city, and swung herself down into the dark, stone tunnel.

The voice of the great Metropolis roared above her. "Danger!" it cried. The stones around her sounded as though they were yawning, and a scratching noise came from about her head. It seemed that the stones themselves were coming to life.

Ahead of her, Maria saw a light as bright as a bonfire. A thousand candles burned in the chamber, a place Maria knew well. In the past she had often stood there and spoken to those whom she called her brothers. Who, but she, had the right to light the candles? For whom were they lit today?

As Maria ran, the walls of the underground city shook right down to the center of the earth. She ran faster and faster as a curtain of stones came down around her.

Above Maria, in the city of Metropolis, the angry mob streamed through the streets like a twisting caravan. Before them, the woman danced the dance of death. Her eyes shone like two bonfires. She told the crowd to kill the machines, and destroy the city and its society. Like beasts running wild, the workers threw themselves toward the New Tower. Stones shook loose under their feet, and smoke billowed up from the street. Suddenly, the lights of the city went out, and only the white, shining clocks hung as patches of light in the darkness.

Metropolis had a brain. Metropolis had a heart, and the heart of the city was a machine. It gave power to all the other machines in Metropolis. This machine was guarded by one man called Grot, who loved his machine above all things. If all the jewelry and every herb and spice in the world were set before him, Grot would still never have parted with his machine.

At sunrise, Grot saw the caravan of angry workers streaming toward the New Tower. He set the lever of the machine on SAFETY, locked the door, and waited for word from Joh Fredersen.

The door trembled like a giant drum as the mob threw itself against it again and again, but Grot smiled to himself, for he knew the door would hold a long time.

The mob wound itself up into a storm. "Open the door!" they yelled. "Death to the machines!"

A bright light shone three times under the dome of the building, and a sound signal could be heard above all the noise. A voice said slowly and clearly, "Grot, open the door and give up the machine!"

Grot shook his head from side to side. "I will not! Not for all the money, jewelry, spices and herbs in the world. Who is speaking?"

"This is Joh Fredersen," said the voice.

Grot could not believe it. "I want the secret word," he insisted.

"The secret word is one thousand and three. Now open the door and give up the machine!"

Grot had no choice. He staggered to the door and pulled it open as the mob screamed with joy. The dancing woman led them toward the machine, but Grot jumped in front of it. To the mob, the man and the machine became one, so if they destroyed him, they destroyed the machine. They seized him, stepped upon him, and dragged him out the door.

The crowd did not notice that their woman leader was not with them. She was standing in front of the Heart-machine of the city. She stretched out her hand, grabbed the lever, which was at SAFETY, and with a cool smile, turned the lever completely around. The machine raced and roared as the temperature of Metropolis began to rise to a dangerous level.

The Heart-Machine

COMPREHENSION CHECK

Choose the best answer.

1. Freder ran to
   _____ a. Rotwang's house.
   _____ b. find Maria.
   _____ c. see his father.
   _____ d. get a doctor for Georgi.

2. It sounded to Maria as if the machines were crying,
   _____ a. "Help!"
   _____ b. "Danger!"
   _____ c. "Maria!"
   _____ d. "Open the door!"

3. Maria was able to escape from Rotwang's house because
   _____ a. Joh Fredersen had killed Rotwang.
   _____ b. Freder came to rescue her.
   _____ c. she found a new way out.
   _____ d. the house was on fire.

4. The heart and brain of Metropolis was
   _____ a. a great fire.
   _____ b. the workers.
   _____ c. a machine.
   _____ d. Futura, the creature.

5. The man named Grot
   _____ a. was the leader of the angry workers.
   _____ b. wanted to destroy the machines.
   _____ c. would do anything for money.
   _____ d. loved his machine more than anything.

6. Joh Fredersen told Grot to
   _____ a. open the door.
   _____ b. close the door.
   _____ c. turn on the machine.
   _____ d. turn off the machine.

7. First, Grot jumped in front of the machine. Then, the workers dragged him away. Next,
   _____ a. Grot staggered to the door.
   _____ b. Joh Fredersen said the secret word.
   _____ c. the woman grabbed the lever.
   _____ d. the machine raced and roared.

8. When the lever was turned off SAFETY,
   _____ a. the temperature began to rise.
   _____ b. the machine exploded.
   _____ c. the whistle blew.
   _____ d. the machine stopped running.

9. Another name for this story could be
   _____ a. "Another Machine."
   _____ b. "The Most Important Machine."
   _____ c. "A Broken Heart."
   _____ d. "Words From the Heart."

10. This story is mainly about
    _____ a. Grot's feelings.
    _____ b. the noise of the machines.
    _____ c. Maria's flight.
    _____ d. the danger in Metropolis.

Check your answers with the key on page 67.

52

Preview Answer:

a. Freder had to try and save Metropolis.

The Heart-Machine

VOCABULARY CHECK

bonfire	caravan	herb	jewelry	society	stationary

I. Sentences to Finish

Fill in the blank in each sentence with the correct key word from the box above.

1. My mother used a special _____ to make the chicken taste so good.

2. Every _____ has rules, but the rules are not all the same.

3. Jack brought the hose in case the _____ got out of control.

4. The rich woman sold all her _____ and gave away the money.

5. The trip was halted until the _____ could be repaired.

6. When the children were sure the rock was _____ ,they used it as a stepping stone across the stream.

II. Making Sense of Sentences

Are the statements below true or false? Put an X next to the correct answer.

1. A <u>caravan</u> is a delicious kind of candy. _____ True _____ False

2. If you go too near a <u>bonfire</u>, you might get burned. _____ True _____ False

3. Someone might put an <u>herb</u> in your dinner. _____ True _____ False

4. You have to run fast to catch up with a <u>stationary</u> object. _____ True _____ False

5. A group of doctors or dog lovers might be called a <u>society</u>. _____ True _____ False

6. People wear <u>jewelry</u> to keep them dry on a rainy day. _____ True _____ False

Check your answers with the key on page 71.

City of Terror

PREPARATION

Key Words

bronze	(bronz)	a metal made from copper and tin *The bronze statue has a red-brown color.*
canal	(kə nal′)	a body of water made especially for travel *The boat floated down the canal.*
cement	(sə ment′)	building material used for holding stones or bricks together *The builders used cement to repair the sidewalk.*
conquer	(kong′ kər)	to get control of; to overcome *The strong can usually conquer the weak.*
crumble	(krum′ bəl)	to break into smaller pieces *The cookie will crumble if you step on it.*
generation	(jen ə rā′ shən)	a group of people born and living during the same period of time *My grandmother and grandfather are from the same generation, but I'm not.*

City of Terror

Necessary Words

destruction	(di struk' shən)	to pull down or wreck something; to destroy *Fires and floods cause much destruction to our lands.*
greed	(grēd)	wanting to get more than one's share *The greed of each man did not allow him to share friendship.*

City of Terror

The workers rushed to kill Maria, for they thought she was the creature who led them in the terrible destruction of Metropolis.

Preview:
1. Read the name of the story.
2. Look at the picture.
3. Read the sentence under the picture.
4. Read the first three paragraphs of the story.
5. Then answer the following question.

You learned from your preview that
_____ a. the lever was set too low.
_____ b. the lever was set on SAFETY.
_____ c. the lever had never been so high.
_____ d. the lever was set on 6.

Turn to the Comprehensive Check on page 58 for the right answer.

Now read the story.

Read to find out if Maria and the city of Metropolis can be saved.

City of Terror

One bronze lever controlled the life of all the machines in the city of Metropolis. When the lever was on SAFETY, the machines would play like tame animals. When the lever was at six, the machines would roar, "Work!" Now the lever was set at twelve. Never in the history of Metropolis had it been set so high.

The city began to run a temperature, and the heat spread through the cement streets and stone buildings, causing some to quiver and others to crumble.

Freder found his father alone in the New Tower. "Father, your city and its people are dying. You must do something to save them!" cried Freder.

Joh Fredersen just smiled and said, "Destruction has come upon the city by my own wish. I have come to realize that the city was built on greed. The city must die so that you, and the generation after you,may build it again."

Down in the tunnel in the City of the Dead, Maria felt something licking at her feet like the tongue of a great,gentle dog. She bent down and felt that it was water.

At one time,a canal wound its way deep under Metropolis, but Joh Fredersen walled it up when he built the underground city for the workmen of Metropolis. Now the walls were starting to crumble and the water was beginning to flow.

The water grew deeper and deeper as Maria dragged her dripping body over cement blocks. She finally found the door that led up from the tunnel to the workmen's underground city. Maria pulled herself up through the door and saw the empty streets and dimming lights of the square.

Suddenly, the bronze door through which she had come, flew open, and water rushed up and ran across the smooth streets. The lights of the workmen's city flickered as the water wound its way through the streets like a dark, crawling beast.

Maria gathered the wandering children and led them up many sets of steps toward the city of Metropolis which stood above. The door to the street would not open and it seemed as though the water would conquer Maria and the children. Just in time, Freder arrived and helped them all up into the street of Metropolis. Then the children were taken to the Club of the Sons to be cared for and kept safe.

Gangs of people ran through the streets, shouting and howling, wild with excitement. Maria's eyes found the New Tower of Babel and she knew she had to go there to see Joh Fredersen. But Maria never went.

Suddenly, the air turned blood-red from a thousand torches. The torches danced in the hands of people whose faces shone with madness. The flaming parade was led by a woman who screamed with Maria's voice, "Dance the dance of death!"

The woman crossed the torches above her head like swords. Then she swung them right and left so that showers of sparks flew around her. Jan, Freder's old friend, ran alongside the woman he thought was Maria. He called out to her, but the woman struck him in the face with her sparkling club. The man's clothes caught fire, but he still ran beside her.

Then, the door of the church opened and the monk Desertus came out, leading his own parade. Its members wore black robes, walked on bare feet, and carried heavy whips which they swung from side to side.

"The sins of the generations are bringing destruction to the city!" shouted the monks.

Maria looked at the madness around her and knew she had to run to get away. The streets flew by her in a whirl and soon she saw another wild mob flowing toward her like a twisting canal.

These people were wearing the dark clothes of the workers, so she stretched out her arms and called to them, "Brothers and Sisters!"

But a wild roar answered her as the mob came rushing at her. "There she is; the one who is to blame for everything. Take her!" they cried. "Burn the witch before we are all destroyed!"

Maria turned and ran in blind horror as stones flew at her from behind. She realized that she was headed back to the church. Maria threw herself forward with her last bit of strength. She stumbled up the steps of the church, fell through the door into the welcome darkness, and saw the soft,flickering candles.

Maria did not see the stream of dancers and workers meet angrily outside. She did not even hear the shouts of the mob as they built the bonfire in front of the church to burn the witch. Sleep had conquered her.

"Freder! Grot!" shouted Josephat, so that his voice cracked through the machine rooms of the New Tower. He banged on the door to the machine room, where the wounded machines were howling. Grot finally answered.

"Out of my way!" shouted Josephat. "Where is Freder?"

"I am here," came the reply. "What is the matter?"

"Freder, they have taken Maria prisoner and they are going to kill her!" Josephat explained.

Freder ran out the door and jumped into the little car in which Josephat had come. His face shone like a white stone and his eyes burned like jewels.

City of Terror

COMPREHENSION CHECK

Choose the best answer.

1. Joh Fredersen wanted the city to die so
   _____ a. it could never be built again.
   _____ b. it could be built again.
   _____ c. he could show that he was boss.
   _____ d. the workers would be punished.

2. First, Maria gathered up the children. Then, she led them up the steps toward the city. Next,
   _____ a. Freder helped her open the door.
   _____ b. the door flew open.
   _____ c. the children were taken to the Club of the Sons.
   _____ d. Maria felt something licking her feet.

3. The parade of flaming torches was led by
   _____ a. the children.
   _____ b. Maria.
   _____ c. Futura, the creature.
   _____ d. Desertus, the monk.

4. The black-robed marchers carrying whips were led by
   _____ a. the children.
   _____ b. Maria.
   _____ c. Futura, the creature.
   _____ d. Desertus, the monk.

5. Maria called to the workers because
   _____ a. she wanted to join their parade.
   _____ b. they were going the wrong way.
   _____ c. she thought they were her friends.
   _____ d. she wanted to stir up trouble.

6. The workers rushed at Maria calling,
   _____ a. "Where is Freder?"
   _____ b. "Save us!"
   _____ c. "Come with us!"
   _____ d. "Burn the witch!"

7. With the crowd behind her, Maria stumbled up the steps and went inside
   _____ a. the church.
   _____ b. the New Tower.
   _____ c. the City of the Dead.
   _____ d. the machine room.

8. Josephat ran to tell Freder that the crowd was
   _____ a. running wild in the streets.
   _____ b. going to kill Maria.
   _____ c. coming to get him.
   _____ d. destroying the city.

9. Another name for this story could be
   _____ a. "A Terrible Enemy."
   _____ b. "City of Steel."
   _____ c. "Metropolis in Danger."
   _____ d. "A Brave Deed."

10. This story is mainly about
   _____ a. how the children were rescued.
   _____ b. the route Maria took to the church.
   _____ c. the terrible things happening in the city.
   _____ d. how a witch destroyed Metropolis.

Check your answers with the key on page 67.

City of Terror

VOCABULARY CHECK

bronze	canal	cement	conquer	crumble	generation

I. Sentences to Finish

Fill in the blank in each sentence with the correct key word from the box above.

1. The steps in front of our house are made of _____ .

2. If you swam in the _____ , you might get hit by a boat.

3. My mother and my aunt are members of the same _____ .

4. The wood is so old, it will _____ if you touch it.

5. Scientists are working hard to _____ diseases.

6. Long ago, people learned to make tools of iron and _____ .

II. Crossword Puzzle

Fill in the puzzle with the key words from the box above. Use the meanings below to help you choose the right word.

Down

1. a metal

2. building material

6. get control of

Across

3. break into pieces

4. body of water made for travel

5. group of people born during the same period of time

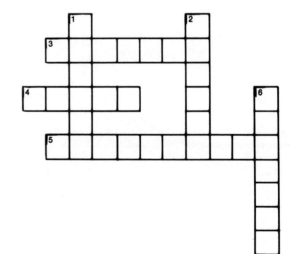

Check your answers with the key on page 71.

A New Dawn for Metropolis

PREPARATION

Key Words

attempt	(ə tempt′)	to try to do something *If I never attempt this trick, I'll never know if I can do it.*
breeches	(brē′ chiz)	trousers that end just below the knee *Long ago, men and boys wore brightly colored breeches.*
chant	(chant)	to speak or sing with a steady, even beat *The Indians began to chant their praises to the sun.*
dart	(därt)	to run quickly *Did you see that deer dart behind the trees as we drove up?*
proper	(prop′ ər)	correct; well-mannered *It is not proper to come to the dinner table with dirty hands.*
thrilling	(thril′ ing)	very exciting *That roller coaster ride was thrilling!*

A New Dawn for Metropolis

Necessary Words

tattered	(tat′ ərd)	full of tatters; torn; ragged

After the heavy winds, the flag hung <u>tattered</u> upon the mast.

A New Dawn for Metropolis

Joh Fredersen cried as he watched his son carrying Maria from the church tower. And the creature, Futura, burned in the bonfire.

Preview:
1. Read the name of the story.
2. Look at the picture.
3. Read the sentences under the picture.
4. Read the first two paragraphs of the story.
5. Then answer the following question.

You learned from your preview that
_____ a. the crowd caught a woman outside the church.
_____ b. the crowd caught a woman inside the church.
_____ c. a woman escaped the crowd near the church.
_____ d. the crowd burned down the church.

Turn to the Comprehension Check on page 64 for the right answer.

Now read the story.

Read to find out how Freder and the workers of Metropolis realize that a false Maria tricked them.

A New Dawn for Metropolis

In the tiny car, Freder and Josephat wound their way through broken streets.

"I don't know how it happened that Maria fell into their hands," sighed Josephat. "I was on my way to you, when I saw a woman running across the church square in an attempt to escape the mob. They wanted to kill her, for they believed she was responsible for the destruction of the city. She didn't reach the church. She fell on the steps and they caught her there. I heard them chant, 'Burn the witch!' as they began to build a bonfire."

Freder said nothing as the car groaned and jumped.

"Freder," cried Josephat, "we can't get through this way. The bridge is gone!"

"But we must!" screamed Freder. "Don't you hear the chanting?"

The sky in the distance was turning bright red. Freder stared at the ribbons of iron which were dangling from the torn bridge. He thought he could attempt to dart across the one beam of the bridge that was still connected to the two sides of the street.

The little car moved over the beam, which gave out a screeching sound as the rubber tires slid across it. Suddenly, the car shot forward and turned over, as the dying beam crashed into empty space. Freder got up, but Josephat remained still on the ground. He lifted his head and told Freder to think only of Maria and run.

Freder dashed through streets and up stairs, until at last he came upon the church square. People danced madly and swung torches around a pile of wood. Tied to the top of the wood was the woman Freder believed to be Maria.

The woman raised her head and her eyes found Freder. She smiled and her voice flew through the roar of the mob. "Dance with me my darling," she hissed.

The mob recognized Freder as Joh Fredersen's son, and they began to scream. They tried to grab him, but he darted past.

"Why do you want to kill her?" Freder cried. "Kill me if you must, but please let her live."

"Each in his own proper turn, son of Joh Fredersen," one said. "But first you shall see your loved one die a thrilling, hot death."

A woman tore off a strip of her skirt and tied Freder to a post. A wild, red gleam caught Freder's eye as the bonfire flared. The men and women joined hands and danced around the fire faster and faster. "Burn the witch!" they chanted.

Freder struggled so hard his bonds broke, and he fell to the ground among the feet of the dancers. He looked up and saw the woman's hair and gown blazing. A lovely smile showed on her mouth as she shouted to him through the flames, "Dance with me, my dearest."

High in the tower window of the church, a white form fluttered like a bird. Maria gazed out the window and saw Freder far below. He lay on the ground near the bonfire, his breeches torn and his forehead in the dust.

"Freder, help me," she screamed.

Freder darted up as if he were being whipped. "I am coming, Maria!" he cried.

All those who danced around the bonfire saw the girl who had fallen and was now hanging from the tower of the church.

Joh Fredersen stood in the board room of the New Tower, waiting for news about his son. A ghostly darkness hung over the New Tower. The lights of the city had gone out at the moment the huge Heart-machine of Metropolis came free from its platform.

Joh Fredersen had been standing a long time in the same spot, not able to move. Then the door of the room flew open and Slim entered, his eyes wide.

"I have not found your son," said Slim. "Do you know, Mr. Fredersen, what is going on around you?" he asked in a shrill, thrilling voice.

"What is happening is what is proper," said Fredersen.

Slim jumped forward like a beast ready to attack Joh Fredersen. "It means Freder is not to be found because he had to see with his own eyes exactly what his father is allowing to happen to Metropolis. It means that Freder has left the safety of his home and is in a city in which madness is running wild," said Slim sternly.

Joh Fredersen put his hands to his head and cried out the name of his son in a soft voice.

Meanwhile, Josephat, for whom every step meant pain, crept up the stairs of the New Tower. "Freder has been captured by the mob!" he shouted as he entered the room.

Fredersen flung himself through the door and ran through the broken streets of Metropolis. Soon he came to the church square, where the creature of metal and glass stood melting in the bonfire. His eyes turned upward and found a man in a torn, silk shirt and tattered breeches walking along the roof of the church. It was Freder, and in his arms he carried Maria.

Joh Fredersen bent down so low that his head touched the stones on the church square. Those near enough to him heard the weeping that rose from his heart. His son was safe.

The mob fell silent. The destruction was over, and a new dawn would bring a new light to the city of Metropolis.

A New Dawn for Metropolis

COMPREHENSION CHECK

Choose the best answer.

1. Freder got across the broken bridge by
   _____ a. running and jumping over.
   _____ b. connecting the beams.
   _____ c. driving across one beam.
   _____ d. leaving Josephat behind.

2. When Freder reached the church square, he saw
   _____ a. his father.
   _____ b. Josephat.
   _____ c. a woman tied to the church tower.
   _____ d. a woman tied on top of a pile of wood.

3. First, the crowd recognized Freder. Then, they tied him to a post. Next,
   _____ a. Maria called to him.
   _____ b. a woman tore off a strip of her skirt.
   _____ c. Freder broke free.
   _____ d. Freder ran to help Maria.

4. The white form that fluttered in the tower window was
   _____ a. the real Maria.
   _____ b. Futura, the creature.
   _____ c. Freder.
   _____ d. a bird.

5. Josephat told Joh Fredersen that
   _____ a. Freder had left home.
   _____ b. Freder had been captured.
   _____ c. Freder was safe.
   _____ d. Freder was on the roof of the church.

6. The woman in the bonfire was
   _____ a. Maria.
   _____ b. a witch.
   _____ c. the woman who tore her skirt.
   _____ d. Futura, the creature who looked like Maria.

7. Freder went up the church tower to
   _____ a. get away from the crowd.
   _____ b. capture the creature.
   _____ c. rescue Maria.
   _____ d. frighten his father.

8. Joh Fredersen wept because
   _____ a. he was sorry that Freder was safe.
   _____ b. he was glad that Freder was safe.
   _____ c. the city had not been destroyed.
   _____ d. he hurt his head on the stones.

9. Another name for this story could be
   _____ a. "Freder at the Bridge."
   _____ b. "An End to the Madness."
   _____ c. "The Strength of Metropolis."
   _____ d. "A City Without Hope."

10. This story is mainly about
    _____ a. how Maria is saved.
    _____ b. burning a witch.
    _____ c. how peace returns to Metropolis.
    _____ d. the future of Metropolis.

Check your answers with the key on page 67.

A New Dawn for Metropolis

VOCABULARY CHECK

attempt	breeches	chant	dart	proper	thrilling

I. Sentences to Finish

Fill in the blank in each sentence with the correct key word from the box above.

1. Our grandfather told us he wore _____ when he was a boy.

2. Amy knows it is _____ to say please and thank you.

3. Chipmunks _____ away when you come near them.

4. Uncle Joe told us about his _____ adventures in the jungle.

5. Mike will _____ to jump even higher that he did before.

6. Children sometimes _____ funny rhymes when they skip rope.

II. Matching

Write the letter of the correct meaning from Column B next the key word in Column A.

Column A	Column B
_____ 1. attempt	a. exciting
_____ 2. breeches	b. correct
_____ 3. chant	c. to try
_____ 4. dart	d. to speak with a steady beat
_____ 5. proper	e. knee-length trousers
_____ 6. thrilling	f. to run quickly

Check your answers with the key on page 72.

NOTES

COMPREHENSION CHECK ANSWER KEY

Lessons CTR E-1 to CTR E-10

LESSON NUMBER	QUESTION NUMBER										PAGE NUMBER
	1	2	3	4	5	6	7	8	9	10	
CTR E-1	d	c	b	b	d	a	b	b	c	c	10
CTR E-2	b	a	c	d	a	b	a	d	a	a	16
CTR E-3	a	b	a	a	c	b	d	a	c	a	22
CTR E-4	c	c	b	d	b	a	c	b	c	d	28
CTR E-5	b	d	a	b	b	d	c	b	a	b	34
CTR E-6	b	c	c	b	b	d	a	b	b	d	40
CTR E-7	c	d	c	c	b	a	d	c	c	b	46
CTR E-8	c	b	a	c	d	a	c	a	b	d	52
CTR E-9	b	a	c	d	c	d	a	b	c	c	58
CTR E-10	c	d	c	a	b	d	c	b	b	c	64

Code:

◯ = Not said straight out, but you know from what is said.

◇ = Recalling order of events in the story

△ = Another name for the story

▢ = Main idea of the story

NOTES

VOCABULARY CHECK ANSWER KEY
Lessons CTR E-1 to CTR E-10

1 THE MACHINE CITY

I.
1. clumsy
2. purchase
3. boss
4. member
5. ceiling
6. effort

II.
1. c
2. a
3. f
4. e
5. b
6. d

2 FREDER'S DECISION

I.
1. emergency
2. musical
3. concert
4. admission
5. hum
6. melody

II.
1. musical
2. hum
3. emergency
4. concert
5. admission
6. melody
   master

3 A STRANGE VISIT

I.
1. flung
2. bough
3. dense
4. timber
5. crush
6. monster

II.
1. False
2. True
3. True
4. False
5. False
6. True

VOCABULARY CHECK ANSWER KEY
Lesson CTR E-1 to CTR E-10

**Lesson
Number**

**Page
Number**

4 **THE CITY OF THE DEAD** 29

I. 1. pal
2. sturdy
3. aisle
4. recess
5. invisible
6. mask

II.

```
      ¹M
       A
  ²S T U ³R D Y
   K     E     ⁴P ⁵A L
         C        I
         E        S
         S        L
  ⁶I N V I S I B L E
```

5 **FIGHTING AGAINST A DREADFUL POWER** 35

I. 1. value
2. clutch
3. junk
4. pace
5. hasty
6. dodge

II.
```
A M H T P O J K D O
G P A V A L U E O H
N E R U C H N A C E
D O D G E A K J L U
T U V A N L E G U A
O J U E T H A S T Y
C E D O G N U E C L
V A U H O D C S H T
```

6 **DIFFICULT TIMES** 41

I. 1. capital
2. spaghetti
3. garment
4. alter
5. geography
6. appreciate

II. 1. appreciate
2. spaghetti
3. garment
4. capital
5. alter
6. geography
   a smile

VOCABULARY CHECK ANSWER KEY
Lessons CTR E-1 to CTR E-10

Lesson Number		Page Number
7	**THE DANCE OF DEATH**	47

I.
1. furious
2. chamber
3. compact
4. system
5. practical
6. peculiar

II.
1. chamber
2. peculiar
3. practical
4. system
5. compact
6. furious

8	**THE HEART-MACHINE**	53

I.
1. herb
2. society
3. bonfire
4. jewelry
5. caravan
6. stationary

II.
1. False
2. True
3. True
4. False
5. True
6. False

9	**CITY OF TERROR**	59

I.
1. cement
2. canal
3. generation
4. crumble
5. conquer
6. bronze

II.

```
        ¹B              ²C
  ³C  R  U  M  B  L  E
        O              M
⁴C  A  N  A  L         E        ⁶C
        Z              N        O
        ⁵G  E  N  E  R  A  T  I  O  N
                                Q
                                U
                                E
                                R
```

Lesson Number			Page Number

10   **A NEW DAWN FOR METROPOLIS**   65

I. 1. breeches   II. 1. c
    2. proper   2. e
    3. dart   3. d
    4. thrilling   4. f
    5. attempt   5. b
    6. chant   6. a